Sam Spud, Private Eye

by Maureen Ulrich

Baker's Plays
7611 Sunset Blvd.
Los Angeles, CA 90042
bakersplays.com

FEMALE CHARACTERS

JANE REYNOLDS – Sam's down-to-earth secretary; the brains behind his operation

LULA BAUM-SCHELL – gorgeous former starlet; now married to Edward Baum-Schell

PHOEBE BAUM-SCHELL – Edward's daughter; home from private boarding school

DORIS – Danny's wife

MARTHA – Edward's elderly housekeeper; very proper British accent

LIGHT FINGERS LAVERNE – female pickpocket; gangster accent

MALE CHARACTERS

SAM SPUD – down-on-his-luck private eye; has a junk food problem

INSPECTOR OISEAU – police inspector; speaks with a corny French accent

JUNIOR – Edward's son; in college; scrawny; speaks with a lisp

DANNY – owns the Greasy Spoon cafe; a little greasy himself; Sam's informant

EDWARD BAUM-SCHELL – fabulously wealthy owner of Barfy's Dogfood; arrogant

POLICE CONSTABLE

SUPERINTENDENT – wants Sam to pay his office rent

SECOND STORY SID – thief; gangster accent

BENNY THE FENCE – sells stuff that Laverne and Sid steal; more refined than Benny or Laverne

Scene One

(Sam's office. Evening.)

*(**SAM** is sitting in his chair at right with his feet up on his desk. He is reading a newspaper and eating Doritos. There is a coat rack at far left. A window is located at center. The general atmosphere of Sam's office is shabby.)*

SAM. *(addressing the audience)* It was a rainy Tuesday night in the city. It was late. I was alone in my crummy office – as usual. My secretary had gone home several hours earlier. I had nothing to go home to anymore since my fish died and my cat ran away. The city can be a lonely place. I was working on my third bag of Doritos when I heard a knock at the door.

(knock)

SAM. I didn't answer it. It was late and I didn't feel like facing another desperate woman who wanted her cheating schnook of a husband followed – or –

SUPERINTENDENT. Spud, I know you're in there!

SAM. *(desperately putting the newspaper over his head)* Or the super coming to collect the rent!

SUPERINTENDENT. Open up, Spud! You owe me three hundred bucks! That's four months rent, you lousy bum!

*(**SAM** gets up and darts about, looking for a place to hide.)*

SAM. Ever since I lost my police badge, my life had been sliding downhill faster than a couple of fat guys on a toboggan. My life stank like a pair of old running shoes in a gym locker.

SUPERINTENDENT. I'm going to get my keys, Sam! And then I'm gonna open this door and you're gonna wish you'd never been born!

SAM. *(going to the window)* Fortunately, there was a crummy fire escape right outside my crummy window that overlooked the crummy back alley. *(begins to raise leg as if to climb out the window)*

(lighter knock)

(SAM freezes.)

JANE. Sam, it's me – Jane! Let me in!

(SAM straightens up and adjusts his tie.)

SAM. I recognized the voice of my secretary, Jane Reynolds. The crazy kid's had a crush on me ever since I hired her two weeks ago.

JANE. *(impatiently)* Sam! I can hear you talking to yourself again! Will you unlock the door please? I'm soaking wet!

(SAM goes over to the door, and opens it. JANE enters, carrying an umbrella and wearing a trench coat. She shakes out the umbrella.)

SAM. *(looking over her shoulder nervously)* What are you doing back here, kid? It's a nasty night for a doll like you to be out on the street.

JANE. I was going bowling with some of my girlfriends, and I saw the light was on in your office. I ducked out at a red light. *(She takes off the coat and hangs it up on the coat rack)*. Sam, why are you still here? You haven't had a case in two weeks.

SAM. I'm a little low on cash at the moment, but I'm expecting some cheques in the mail any day now. *(opens the door and looks down the hallway)*

JANE. Sam, I'm going to ask you a question and I want an honest answer. Sam, look at me!

(SAM slowly turns and faces her.)

JANE. Sam, are you sleeping here at night?

SAM. Of course not!

JANE. *(walking to his desk)* You've been kicked out of your apartment, haven't you?

SAM. How did you know?

(*JANE opens his desk drawer and pulls out a teddy bear.*)

SAM. Hey, give me Binky! (*grabs teddy out of* JANE*'s hand*)

JANE. Sam, you need a case. As near as I can tell – from looking at your account books – which are in pathetic shape I might add – you don't have any money coming. Your bank account is bone dry. You can't even afford to pay me. (*pauses*) You need help.

SAM. Do not!

JANE. Why don't you call some of your friends down at the police station and get a lead on someone who might need a private eye? Maybe you could talk to Inspector Oiseau.

SAM. Never! And don't you ever mention that name in this office again! Do you hear me? (*opens his desk drawer, pulls out a new bag of Doritos, and rips it open*) Oiseau ruined my life – took away my badge! If it wasn't for him, I'd still be on the force!

JANE. (*tears the Doritos out of his hand*) Sam, you can't keep doing this to yourself! Don't you care what happens to you?

SAM. (*takes the Doritos back*) No, I don't. And neither should you, kid. I'm no good for you. (*wipes the back of his hand against his mouth*) I'm poison, kid.

(*Knock.*)

SAM. (*hiding under his desk*) It must be the superintendant! Tell him I'm not here!

JANE. Sam, you can't run away from your problems! You have to face them like a man!

(*SAM's arm reaches out from beneath the desk and grabs Binky.*)

JANE. You are hopeless! (*walks to the door and opens it*)

(*LULA enters, wearing a mink stole and a veiled hat and carrying an umbrella.*)

LULA. You aren't Sam Spud, are you?

JANE. No, of course not, I'm his secretary. Jane Reynolds. Did you want to see Sam?

LULA. *(looking disdainfully around the office)* I'm not so sure. Is he available?

JANE. *(sarcastically)* Oh, he's available, all right. May I ask who you are?

LULA. *(turns to face* JANE, *her back to the desk)* I'm Lula Baum-Schell. Didn't you recognize me?

JANE. Lula Baum-Schell? THE Lula Baum-Schell?

(SAM's head abruptly appears from beneath the desk and stares at LULA in amazement.)

LULA. *(opens her purse and takes out a small mirror and lipstick)* I thought that my name might…ring a bell. *(begins outlining her lips)*

JANE. You're a famous model from Vogue magazine who achieved instant stardom when you starred opposite Humphrey Bogart in two detective movies.

SAM. Wow!

JANE. But recently you married that millionaire – what's his name again?

LULA. Edward Northrop Baum-Schell. The Barfy's dogfood tycoon.

JANE. *(snapping her fingers)* That's it!

LULA. Look, I'm really enjoying all this small talk, but I'm here to see the detective, understand? If he's not here right now, I'll come back another time. *(moves to leave)*

(SAM crawls out from behind desk, teddy bear under his left arm, and hurries across the room.)

SAM. Mrs. Baum-Schell, I'm Sam Spud. *(shakes her hand eagerly)* Do you need a private investigator?

LULA. *(looks at him uncertainly)* That depends on your rates. *(notices Binky)* Is that a teddy bear under your arm?

(SAM is at a loss for words.)

JANE. *(interjecting)* It was a clue in your last case, wasn't it, Sam? A fortune in diamonds was hidden in that bear.

The family that had inherited those diamonds didn't know where to look for them, but Sam figured it out. He's a brilliant detective, Mrs. Baum-Schell. *(takes bear from* **SAM** *and puts it on the desk)*

LULA. Then you're just the man I'm looking for, Mr. Spud.

SAM. Call me Sam. And may I call you Doll-face?

LULA. Not on your life.

*(***SUPERINTENDENT*** *enters, carrying a ring of keys.* **LULA** *immediately turns her back to him and faces the window.)*

SUPERINTENDENT. Ah ha! I knew you were here, Spud! Now where's my rent for the past three months?

JANE. Excuse me, Mr. Schwartz, but Sam and I are in the middle of a very important and sensitive case. Naturally you've heard of Lula Baum-Schell.

SUPERINTENDENT. Of course I've heard of Lula Baum-Schell. I don't see –

*(***LULA*** *turns and faces* **SUPERINTENDENT,** *turning on her considerable charms.)*

SUPERINTENDENT. Lula Baum-Schell!

JANE. I'm sure you'll understand, Mr. Schwartz, if we have to ask you to leave us alone.

SUPERINTENDENT. *(reverently)* I shall never forget you in "The Maltese Puppy," Mrs. Baum-Schell. You were magnificent!

LULA. Thank you.

SUPERINTENDENT. But my absolute favourite was "Dial D for Death."

JANE. *(pushing* **SUPERINTENDENT***)* Yes, yes, Mr. Schwartz. There'll be another time and occasion for pleasantries. In the meantime, Sam and I have a case to solve.

SUPERINTENDENT. *(waving at* **LULA***)* Of course. I understand. I won't interfere. Until we meet again, Mrs. Baum-Schell.

*(***SUPERINTENDENT*** *exits.)*

SAM. Whew! That was close!

JANE. I'll say! Are we really four months behind in the office rent, too?

LULA. Can we get down to business – in private? *(looks meaningfully at* **JANE***)*

SAM. Miss Reynolds is a trusted employee, Mrs. Baum-Schell.

LULA. Look, either she walks or I do, get my drift? *(walks over to window and looks out)* And I don't have much time for games. I may have been followed.

(Behind Lula's back, **SAM** *gestures for* **JANE** *to leave. She is reluctant, but finally goes to the door.)*

JANE. I'll just go powder my nose.

*(***JANE*** exits.)*

SAM. *(sitting down behind his desk)* Sit down, Mrs. Baum-Schell. Tell me why you need a private eye.

*(***LULA*** glances one last time out the window and sits down in the chair next to Sam's desk.)*

LULA. *(meaningfully)* Are you brave, Sam?

*(***SAM*** deposits Binky in his desk drawer before answering.)*

SAM. Danger is my middle name, Mrs. Baum-Schell. Let me tell you about the time I –

LULA. *(impatiently)* I don't have time for any stories, Sam. I just need to know if you're willing to put your life on the line. I'll pay you well, of course.

SAM. Just how well, Mrs. Baum-Schell? *(reaches for his Doritos then thinks better of it)*

LULA. A quarter of a million dollars, Sam. Does that sound like enough?

SAM. *(coughing in surprise)* Not bad.

LULA. Okay, I'll get right to the point. *(checks the door to make sure no one is listening)* My husband has disappeared, Sam.

SAM. *(yawning)* Well, husbands do have a habit or wandering off occasionally. I'm sure he'll come home.

LULA. He went out to his men's club last night, and he never returned. In the morning, a man in a dark sedan delivered this to my housekeeper Martha. *(opens her handbag and pulls out a folded up piece of paper)*

SAM. *(taking the paper from her and reading)* This looks like a ransom note.

LULA. Very good, Sam.

SAM. They want a million dollars – in cash? By midnight tomorrow? Do you have that kind of dough?

LULA. Yes, I do, but it'll take time. And as you can see by the note, I can't go to the police. If I do, they'll kill Eddie! *(pulls out a handerkerchief and blows her nose loudly)*

SAM. Do you have any idea who could be behind this, Mrs. Baum-Schell?

LULA. Please, call me Lula. *(pauses)* No, I don't. My husband is a very powerful man. But he also hates to have bodyguards following him around. When he goes out to his club, he drives himself. Just about anyone could have kidnapped him, if they knew his routine.

SAM. What makes you so sure that they have him, Lula?

LULA. *(reaching into her purse again and pulling out a ring)* This ring was in the envelope with the note. I gave it to Eddie on our first anniversary.

SAM. Wow! *(picks up a magnifying glass and examines the ring more closely)* What a rock!

LULA. You've got to help me, Sam! *(stands up and leans against the edge of the desk)*

SAM. What do you want me to do, Lula?

LULA. I just know that as soon as I pay that ransom, they'll kill Eddie! I don't care about the money, I just want my Eddie back. *(goes back to the window and looks out)* You've got to find my husband before tomorrow night.

SAM. Of course.

LULA. *(turns to face SAM and leans against the window)* They'll kill you – if you're not careful.

SAM. (*reaches into his desk and pulls out a water pistol*) I'm always careful, Lula. Caution is my middle name.

LULA. Didn't you say that danger was your middle name?

SAM. (*thinking*) Yeah – danger and caution. (*shakes the pistol to see if there is any water in it and then sucks on the end*)

LULA. What's your first step?

SAM. Well, I'll go out on the street and talk to some of my informants – you know check the grapevine. Then tomorrow morning I'll stop by your estate and talk to your housekeeper.

LULA. (*leaning over him*) Do you really think you can find my Eddie before tomorrow night?

SAM. Absolutely. Reliability is my –

LULA. Never mind. I better be going.

SAM. Hey, how did you know I'd be here tonight, Lula? It's after hours.

LULA. I have my sources. (*walks to the door and pauses to look back at* **SAM**) I'll see you tomorrow, Sam Spud.

(**LULA** *exits.* **SAM** *pulls a dart gun, a skipping rope, etch-a-sketch, etc. out of his desk.* **JANE** *enters.*)

JANE. Well, what happened?

SAM. (*aiming the dart pistol at her*) We've got a case, kid.

JANE. That's great, Sam! How can I help?

SAM. (*stands up*) It's too dangerous, Doll-face. You better go home.

JANE. Where are you going?

SAM. I'm going to talk to my informants – on the street. And the street is no place for a kid like you. (*walks to the coat rack*)

JANE. You're going to Tin Pan Alley?

SAM. You guessed it, Kid. (*removes coat and stuffs the pockets with items*)

JANE. I don't care what you say, Sam. I'm coming with you.

SAM. Suit yourself, Kid. (*shrugs coat on*) But I still get to wear the coat.

(*Blackout.*)

Scene Two

(Tin Pan Alley. Later that evening.)

(There is a street light is at center. **LIGHT FINGERS LAVERNE, SECOND STORY SID,** *and* **BENNY THE FENCE** *are all standing around the light.)*

LAVERNE. See what I got here, Benny. A gold watch and chain. Genuine Swiss workmanship. *(dangles watch in front of Benny's eyes)*

BENNY. *(reaching for the watch)* Let's have a closer look.

LAVERNE. Nope! The last time you had a closer look, I never saw it again! I don't pick pockets just so you can line yours!

BENNY. *(shaking his head)* Laverne, Laverne, Laverne. Don't you trust me?

SID. No, she don't, Benny, and neither do I. Where's the rest of the dough for that diamond necklace and bracelet you fenced for me last week? I nearly broke my neck getting 'em!

BENNY. *(smoothly)* Is that hostility I hear in your voice, Sid?

*(***OISEAU*** *enters. He has a distinctive birdlike gait.* **LAVERNE** *notices him immediately and stuffs the watch in her pocket, though the chain is still hanging out.)*

LAVERNE. Psst! It's the fuzz!

*(***BENNY*** *and* **SID** *assume innocent expressions.* **OISEAU** *casually does a circuit of the three of them.)*

SID. Evenin', Inspector.

LAVERNE. *(ingratiatingly)* Nice night for a stroll, eh, Inspector? Now that the rain's stopped.

BENNY. Got some business on Tin Pan Alley, Inspector?

OISEAU. *(instantly on edge)* And what's zat supposed to mean, Benny?

BENNY. Nothing, nothing. I was just making polite conversation.

OISEAU. Are you implying zat I'm on zee take, Benny? *(leans in on* **BENNY***)*

BENNY. No, not me, Inspector!

OISEAU. Zere may be dirty cops in zis lousy city, Benny, but I'm not one of zem! Do you hear me!

BENNY. Yep!

OISEAU. Just because I come down here once a week to get a little information – information zat I pay for most generously…

BENNY. Most generously, Inspector!

OISEAU. Doesn't mean I'm not on zee up and up.

BENNY. Naturally!

LAVERNE. *(fingering* **OISEAU***'s sleeve)* That's a fine suit yer wearin', Inspector. Looks like it was custom-fitted.

OISEAU. *(turning on* **LAVERNE***)* You zink I coerced zat tailor down the street into giving me zis suit? You zink I told him I'd get his business licence revoked if he didn't hand it over?

LAVERNE. No, Inspector. I was just admirin' it, is all.

OISEAU. *(noticing the chain hanging out of her pocket)* What's zis?

LAVERNE. What's what?

OISEAU. Zis!

LAVERNE. Zis?

OISEAU. Oui!

LAVERNE. *(uncertainly)* Je ne sais pas?

OISEAU. Well, Laverne, I'm waiting!

LAVERNE. It's a watch fob, Inspector. Fer a watch.

OISEAU. Let me see it!

LAVERNE. The fob – or the watch?

OISEAU. Laverne!

LAVERNE. *(slowly pulling out the watch)* They was a gift, Inspector. From my dear old grannie. She placed 'em in my hands on her death bed and said, "Laverne, I leave this cruel world with peace in my heart just knowin' that you'll look after this precious family heirloom."

OISEAU. *(snatching the watch from her hand)* A likely story! *(opens the watch and examines the inscription)* You say zis was your grandmother's watch, Laverne?

(**LAVERNE** *looks uncertainly at* **BENNY** *and* **SID**, *who nod vigorously.*)

LAVERNE. Yes, my grannie. That's what I said. She gave it to my granddad on their wedding day.

OISEAU. And what was your grandfather's name, Laverne?

(**BENNY** *and* **SID** *peer over* **OISEAU**'s *shoulder.*)

LAVERNE. Well, can't you read it in the watch, Inspector?

OISEAU. *(sighing loudly)* Oui, I can read it. I just want to see if it matches up with your story.

LAVERNE. Well, she had a lot of husbands, you know. I never really was sure which one was my granddad.

OISEAU. Please try.

LAVERNE. I think it was…it was…*(smacking herself in the fore-head)* …I knew it yesterday…it might have been…no, that's not right…I have to *(smacking her forehead repeatedly)* think, think, think…

(**SID** *and* **BENNY** *perform charades behind* **OISEAU**'s *back – pretending to dive, swim, paddle a canoe, and drink out of a glass.*)

LAVERNE. Maybe it was…Water?

(**BENNY** *and* **SID** *nod excitedly and made expanding motions with their hands.*)

LAVERNE. Waaatered? Waaatering? Waaalter?

(**BENNY** *and* **SID** *hug excitedly and jump up and down.*)

LAVERNE. That's it – it was Walter!

(**OISEAU** *hands the watch back to* **LAVERNE** *and exits in disgust.*)

LAVERNE. See you next week, Inspector!

SID. Don't take any wooden nickels, Inspector!

BENNY. And remember to look both ways before you cross the street! *(to* **LAVERNE***)* Are you going to let me fence that watch for you now?

LAVERNE. Naw. I've got something much more interesting.

SID. And what's that?

LAVERNE. *(reaching into her other pocket and producing a police badge)* What do you reckon this is worth?

SID. *(admiringly)* Laverne, you got nerves of steel – and hands of solid gold!

LAVERNE. *(proudly)* Don't I though!

BENNY. I know some people who would be very interested in one of those. *(reaches for the badge)*

LAVERNE. *(slapping* **BENNY***'s hand away)* Get yer paws off! I'm savin' this one fer a rainy day!

(The three of them begin to argue heatedly about what to do with the badge.)

*(***SAM*** and* **JANE** *enter.)*

JANE. This place gives me the creeps, Sam.

*(***SID*** notices* **SAM** *and* **JANE** *then mimes getting Laverne's and Benny's attention.)*

SAM. I told you not to come. But since you're here – better stick close. I know this street and the people who live on it like the back of my hand.

JANE. You do?

SAM. One thing you need to realize about me, Kid, is my mind is like a steel trap.

JANE. It is?

SAM. I never forget a face.

*(***LAVERNE*** carefully backs towards* **SAM***.)*

SAM. Yeah, Kid, I know every trick in the book and every – Hey!

*(***LAVERNE*** bumps into* **SAM***.)*

SAM. Hey, it's – *(snaps his fingers)* – now don't tell me – I know you.

JANE. I thought you said that you never forget a face.

SAM. I don't. I remember her face. I just can't think of her name.

LAVERNE. *(holding her hands behind her back)* Marilyn Munroe.

(**BENNY** *and* **SID** *point at* **LAVERNE***'s hands and snicker.)*

SAM. *(shaking a finger at her)* Right, Marilyn. I remember you.

JANE. Sam, Marilyn Munroe is a famous movie star.

SAM. Can't you see I'm busy right now, Jane. *(turns back to* **LAVERNE***)* Now, Marilyn, you work at Woolworth's, don't you?

LAVERNE. Right you are, Sam. At the sock counter.

SAM. I knew it!

SID. Lookin' for information, Sammy?

SAM. *(looking important)* That's right, Syl.

SID. That's Sid, Sam.

SAM. Whatever. *(flips him a quarter)* Got any tips for me, Syl?

SID. *(disgusted)* Always wear clean underwear.

SAM. *(thinking)* Okay. That's good advice.

BENNY. *(surprised)* Somebody hired you, Sam?

SAM. *(defensively)* Yeah! And that somebody is Lula Baum-Schell.

(**LAVERNE**, **SID**, *and* **BENNY** *gasp.)*

BENNY. She's bad news, Sam. Bad, bad news.

SID. That dame is dangerous with a capital D.

LAVERNE. I don't want no part of her business.

BENNY. Has she been to see you, Sam? Does she know where you live?

SAM. Well, I don't technically live anywhere just at the moment.

SID. Stay clear of that broad, Sammy. And that's my final word!

(**BENNY, LAVERNE,** *and* **SID** *exit, while* **LAVERNE** *holds up Sam's watch and admires it.*)

JANE. Well, what do you make of that, Sam?

SAM. I guess it's time to head for Chinatown, Kid.

JANE. Chinatown?

SAM. Yeah, Kid. We'll stop in at Danny's Diner. I'll buy you a coffee.

JANE. *(yawning)* It's getting late, Sam.

SAM. *(looks at his wrist)* Funny. I was sure I strapped on Mickey this morning.

JANE. Shouldn't you go home and get some sleep?

SAM. The street's my home now, Kid. And the night's still young. Let's go.

(Blackout.)

Scene Three

(Danny's Diner. Later that evening.)

*(***DANNY*** *is wiping off the counter at right. There are two stools in front of the counter and a till on top of it.* ***DORIS*** *is drying some plates with a dishtowel. Two customers, wearing trench coats and sunglasses are seated at a table at left. The smell of bacon hangs in the air. There is a coat rack at far left.)*

DANNY. Business is pretty slow tonight, Doris. Maybe we should close up and go home. *(yawns and stretches)* My back is killing me.

DORIS. We're open all night, Danny. We can't close up. What if someone needs a cup of coffee? Or a piece of apple pie? We owe it to our clientele to stay open.

DANNY. Ah, Doris, just once can't we go home early? I thought when I quit my job at the warehouse that I'd done my last night shift – and here I am running a lousy greasy spoon on the wrong side of the tracks.

DORIS. This is not a greasy spoon, Danny. It's a restaurant.

*(She turns her back on ***DANNY*** and picks up another plate.)*

*(***SAM*** *and* ***JANE*** *enter.* ***SAM*** *hangs up the coat on the coat rack.)*

DANNY. Hey, look who's here, Doris! It's my old buddy, Sam Spud – the private eye.

SAM. How's business, Danny? *(shakes Danny's hand)*

DANNY. *(looking around)* Booming. Can I get you a coffee?

SAM. *(sits down at the counter and leans his back against it)* Yeah, that'll hit the spot. It's a cold night here in the windy city, Danny. It's a lonely night for a down-on-his-luck detective who –

JANE. Sam, remember what we came here for?

DANNY. *(pouring some coffee in a cup for ***SAM***)* Hey, who's the doll, Sam? New girlfriend?

SAM. Nah, this is Jane Reynolds, my secretary. She's helping me with a case.

DANNY. *(nudging ***SAM*** with his elbow)* Kind of a looker, ain't she, Sammy? But then you always did have an eye for the ladies.

DORIS. Can I get something for you Miss Reynolds? A special tea? An espresso? Perhaps a cappuccino?

JANE. No, thank you. But maybe you can help us. We're investigating a kidnapping.

DORIS. A kidnapping! How exciting!

SAM. Yeah, when you're a private eye, you see it all, Doris. Each day is a sordid journey through this dog-eat-dog world.

JANE. *(impatiently)* Sam, tell them about Mr. Baum-Schell.

DANNY. Baum-Schell? You mean the dog food guy?

SAM. The very one, Danny. And speaking of dolls, you should have seen his wife. Why she was – *(catches Jane's withering look out of the corner of his eye)* Anyway, this Baum-Schell disappeared last night when he went to his men's club. What's the word on the street?

(DANNY and DORIS exchange shrugs.)

DANNY. I haven't heard a thing, Sam.

(Two customers pay their bill and exit.)

SAM. *(smiles knowingly at JANE)* I'll make it worth your while, Danny. We're talking about a lot of dough here.

DANNY. Just how much dough?

SAM. Oh, maybe two bucks. You sure you don't know anything?

DANNY. *(turning his back on SAM and picking up some glasses to wipe)* I'm sure.

JANE. Hmm. So much for your intricate network of informants.

SAM. *(scratching his head)* I don't know. Danny's never let me down before.

DORIS. *(looking nervously at DANNY)* Maybe I could be of some assistance.

DANNY. Doris, don't you go sticking your nose into this!

DORIS. But it's my civic duty, Danny! I owe it to Mr. Baum-Schell.

(**INSPECTOR OISEAU** *enters with his birdlike gait. He stops in his tracks when he sees* **SAM** *at the counter.*)

OISEAU. Spud! What are you doing here? Zere must be a zousand greasy spoons –

DORIS. Restaurants!

OISEAU. Restaurants – in zis city, and you and I both have to walk into zee same one.

SAM. *(standing)* Yeah, it's a crummy world we live in, Oiseau. But it just got crummier the minute you walked in.

(**DANNY** *and* **DORIS** *watch the conversation between* **SAM, JANE,** *and* **OISEAU** *while* **DANNY** *wipes down the counter and* **DORIS** *cleans the table and chairs at left.*)

OISEAU. *(noticing* **JANE***)* What are you doing here?

SAM. You two know each other?

JANE. *(hastily)* We've met before. I did some steno work at the station a few months ago. Right, Inspector?

OISEAU. Oui, but –

JANE. *(interrupting)* Sam, let's go find some other informants. Maybe they can help us. *(takes* **SAM** *by the arm)*

SAM. I have other informants? *(following* **JANE** *towards the door)*

OISEAU. *(to Sam's back)* What, Spud? Leaving so soon? *(pauses)* Are you afraid of – moi?

SAM. *(turning around)* Me, Oiseau? Afraid? I ain't afraid of nothing.

OISEAU. Zat's a double negative, Sam.

SAM. You're for the birds, Oiseau. I have nothing to say to you. *(turns to leave)*

OISEAU. *(smugly)* Word on the street is zat you haven't had a case in weeks, Spud. You're finished. Washed up. You're a lousy at being a private eye – just like you were lousy at being a cop.

SAM. *(stops abruptly)* You're wrong, Oiseau. You don't know how wrong you are.

JANE. *(defensively)* Sam's on a big case.

OISEAU. *(tips his hat)* Jane, I'd sure like to know what you're doing working for a bum like Sam Spud.

JANE. When Sam's solved this case, he'll have a lot of money. A lot more money than you've ever seen.

OISEAU. Oh – and why is zat?

*(**SAM** in the background urges **JANE** to be quiet, but she goes on impulsively.)*

JANE. Does the name Baum-Schell ring a bell?

OISEAU. *(scratching his head)* Hmm, isn't he zee dog-food guy?

JANE. Yes, his wife came to see Sam a few hours ago.

SAM. *(grabbing her arm)* Come on, Jane. We have some other clues to follow up on, remember? Nice seeing you, Oiseau.

OISEAU. His WIFE came to you? *(scratches his head again)* Seems to me I heard somezing about her getting married, but it wasn't to zat Baum-Schell guy.

JANE. Well, you haven't got your facts straight obviously.

OISEAU. *(shrugging)* I guess not. *(to **SAM**)* So what are you up to, Spud?

SAM. Nothing that would interest you, Oiseau.

OISEAU. Nothing illegal, I hope. You've got an eye for trouble.

SAM. Not as much trouble as you do, Oiseau. *(slyly)* Remember the Velveeta Cheese case?

OISEAU. *(abruptly)* I don't want to talk about it. *(His bird-like mannerisms become more exaggerated as he becomes agitated.)*

SAM. *(smiling)* Yeah, you stank up the joint pretty bad that time, didn't you, Oiseau? Had to rely on old Sam Spud to save you! *(angrily)* And then you turned on me! You couldn't stand the thought of the Commissioner finding out about your bumbling, so you framed me and got me kicked off the force!

OISEAU. *(scoffing)* I never had you framed, Spud. You were eating on the job, and you know it! Sure you started off innocently enough – a bag of potato chips at coffee break. But pretty soon you were sneaking in zose big packages of pretzels and popcorn twists – hiding zem in zee bottom drawer and sneaking a handful whenever you had zee chance. Zat's conduct unbefitting an officer, Spud.

(During **OISEAU**'s *tirade,* **SAM** *slumps down on the stool and lays his head on his arms on the counter.* **DANNY** *hands* **SAM** *a bag of Doritos, and* **SAM** *begins eating compulsively.* **JANE** *rushes over to him.)*

JANE. Stop it, Inspector! Stop it! Can't you see what you're doing to him?!

OISEAU. Jane, how many times have you seen Sam sneaking some salty snack zat's loaded with trans fats? *(pauses)* Zee truth hurts, does it not?

SAM. *(looking up)* You're a heel, Oiseau.

*(***DANNY** *and* **DORIS** *gasp and look at one another.)*

OISEAU. *(rolling up his sleeves)* So I'm a heel? Well, I say you're a junkfood junkie. How do you like zem potatoes?

SAM. *(rolling up his sleeves and standing up)* That's all I'm going to take from you, Oiseau. I'm gonna enjoy this. I've been looking forward to it for a long time.

*(***SAM** *and* **OISEAU** *assume fighting poses and circle one another at center menacingly.)*

JANE. *(stepping in between them)* Sam, you can't fight him. You'll just end up in jail for hitting a cop. Then you'll never solve this case. Let's get out of here before it's too late.

SAM. You're right, kid. *(begins rolling down his sleeves)* You're getting off lucky this time, Oiseau.

OISEAU. I think you're zee lucky one, Spud. *(goes to the coat rack and puts the trench coat around his shoulders like a cape)* Got to fly.

*(***OISEAU** *exits.)*

DORIS. *(watching* **OISEAU** *exit)* I didn't want to say anything in front of the inspector. Would this be a good time to tell you what I know?

SAM. Shoot, Doris.

DORIS. Well, as you probably know, I was born with a silver spoon in my mouth.

SAM. *(amazed)* No, I didn't. How did you manage that?

JANE. *(elbowing him in disgust)* She means that she was born rich, Sam! Go on, Doris.

DORIS. Well, Lula Baum-Schell is Edward's fifth wife. His first four wives all died quite mysteriously. One got hit in the head with a mallet during a polo match, and another one drove off a cliff in his Rolls Royce.

SAM. I get the picture. So why are you telling us this?

DORIS. Edward has two teenage children from his earlier marriages – Edward Junior and Phoebe. The gossip is that since he married Lula, he's been planning to remove them from his will and name Lula as his sole heir.

SAM. And?

JANE. Don't you see, Sam? Maybe one of the children had him kidnapped. They obviously have no reason to love him – since he plans to cut them both out of the will. And remember that Lula said that it had to be someone who knew Edward's routine.

SAM. *(snapping his fingers)* You could be right, Jane. They'd certainly have a motive for making some extra dough. Maybe we have time to – *(looks at his wrist)* – oh, right. What time is it, Danny?

DANNY. *(yawning)* It's closing time, Sam.

SAM. I'll drop you off at your place, Jane. Get some sleep. We'll head over to the Baum-Schell Estate first thing in the morning. I'd like to talk to that housekeeper and the rest of the staff. Maybe they can tell us something about Junior and Phoebe.

JANE. Do you think it could be an inside job, Sam?

SAM. You never know, Kid. *(flips a coin at **DANNY**)* Thanks for the conversation. I'll be back.

    (**JANE** *and* **SAM** *exit.*)

DORIS. Do you think Sam'll find Mr. Baum-Schell, Danny?

DANNY. *(shaking his head)* Not a chance.

    (Blackout.)

Scene Four

(Livingroom of the Baum-Schell mansion. Following morning.)

(The furnishings suggest expensive tastes. There is a couch at center and a desk at right with a phone and a lamp on it. A large window with curtains is behind the couch. There is a coat rack at far left.)

*(**PHOEBE** enters, wearing a private school uniform and carrying a book. She sits down at the desk, opens the book, and begins reading. She closes the book suddenly, stands up, and begins pacing.)*

*(**JUNIOR** enters, wearing sweatpants, a university sweatshirt, and a towel around his neck. His hair is wet. He also wears large, dark rimmed glasses.)*

JUNIOR. *(speaking with a lisp)* Phoebe, what's the matter? Why are you up so early? It's not even six thirty.

PHOEBE. *(stops pacing at the sound of his voice)* I couldn't sleep, Eddie. I've been tossing and turning all night, worrying about poor Daddy. Do you think we'll ever see him again?

JUNIOR. Of course we will, Phoebe. You have to believe in miracles.

PHOEBE. *(changing the subject)* Were you working out in the gym?

JUNIOR. Yes, I swam thirty lengths and then used the weight room. Calisthenics helps me take my mind off Dad. *(sits down on the couch)* Have you had breakfast?

PHOEBE. The servants don't seem to be up yet. I think they're used to sleeping in – since Lula doesn't get up until noon.

JUNIOR. *(sarcastically)* Yes, she doesn't seem to have any trouble sleeping, even though Dad's missing. Funny, isn't it?

PHOEBE. *(looking around nervously and putting a finger to her lips)* Ssssh! You never know who's listening in this house!

JUNIOR. You just said that none of the help is awake. Why are you so afraid?

PHOEBE. *(looks out the window)* I don't trust anyone, Eddie. Did I tell you that Daddy phoned me last week and asked me to come home from boarding school? He wouldn't tell me why, but I think that he knew something bad was going to happen!

JUNIOR. *(scratching his head)* He did the same thing to me. I didn't want to come home because the football coach said I might make fourth string for our next game. But Dad sounded so worried.

(**LULA** *enters, unseen, while* **JUNIOR** *is speaking. She is wearing an expensive dressing gown.)*

JUNIOR. It makes you wonder, doesn't it? What did Dad know that he wasn't telling us?

LULA. I can tell you.

PHOEBE. *(whirling)* Lula!

LULA. *(walking towards* **PHOEBE** *and lifting one of her pigtails)* You know that I would prefer you to call me 'Mother.' Why don't you try?

PHOEBE. *(pulling away in distaste)* I'll – I'll think about it.

LULA. *(turning towards* **JUNIOR***)* And the same goes for you of course, Junior. *(runs her hand up the muscle on his arm)* Have you been working out again? Your muscle tone is amazing!

JUNIOR. *(uncomfortably)* Yes, I was just using the pool and weight room. I need to keep in shape for football.

LULA. *(smiling)* Of course you do.

PHOEBE. Did you sleep well – Mother?

LULA. *(sinking down on the sofa)* I'm afraid not. I haven't slept a wink since your father was – since he was – *(pulls a handkerchief out of her sleeve and begins sobbing loudly)*

PHOEBE. *(kneeling beside her)* I'm sorry. I didn't mean to make you cry.

JUNIOR. What was it you said when you came in just now?

That you knew why Dad wanted us to come home?

LULA. *(wiping her eyes)* Yes, I did say that didn't I? *(pulling herself together)* Children, there's something you both should know about your father.

PHOEBE. *(concerned)* What? What is it – Lula, I mean, Mother?

LULA. *(taking both of their hands)* Your father had recently been to the doctor for his annual check-up, and he discovered – *(pauses)* Excuse me, this is just so painful to talk about. *(blows her nose loudly)* Your father learned that he has a bad heart.

PHOEBE. Oh dear!

JUNIOR. A bad heart? But he's as strong as an ox! He works out all the time!

LULA. Well, I'm afraid he was exercising too much. He has overworked his heart and the doctor said he has only a few months to live.

PHOEBE. Poor Daddy!

LULA. This kidnapping will take a frightful toll on his heart! He could drop dead from the strain at any moment!

PHOEBE. *(bursting into tears)* This is terrible!

JUNIOR. *(standing up and going to the phone)* I think we should call the police. I know the kidnappers could kill him – but it's a risk we have to take!

LULA. Junior, how can you be so heartless!

JUNIOR. Well, we have to do something! We can't just sit around and wait for midnight. Once we give the kidnappers the money – who knows what they'll do to Dad? *(turns to **PHOEBE**)* Don't you agree, Phoebe?

PHOEBE. *(wringing her hands)* I don't know, Eddie.

LULA. *(sitting and putting her arm around **PHOEBE**)* We don't need to call the police. I have good news for both of you. I have hired a private detective to find your father.

PHOEBE. *(gasping)* A private eye?

JUNIOR. I hope you got the best that money can buy.

LULA. I can assure you that he's very experienced. I went to see him last night, and he's hot on the trail of your father's kidnappers even as we speak.

(Doorbell chimes.)

LULA. Now who could that be at this time of the morning?

PHOEBE. *(going to the window)* Well, whoever it is just drove up here in a rust-bucket.

JUNIOR. Could it be word from the kidnappers, do you suppose?

*(**MARTHA** enters, wearing a housecoat and slippers.)*

MARTHA. Excuse me, Mrs. Baum-Schell, but there's a man here to see you. He said that you would know him. His name is Sam Spud.

PHOEBE. Sam Spud? Who's that?

LULA. *(smiling brightly)* The man who's going to find your father, Phoebe. *(to **MARTHA**)* Show him in, Martha.

*(**MARTHA** exits.)*

JUNIOR. You're sure this is the man for the job?

LULA. Of course, Junior. He has excellent credentials.

*(**MARTHA** reenters with **SAM** and **JANE**. **SAM** is wearing the trench coat again.)*

MARTHA. May I present Mr. Spud and his associate.

*(**MARTHA** exits)*

LULA. *(stepping forward)* Good morning, Sam. I trust that you have come to bring us the good news of Edward's release?

SAM. *(looking around uncertainly)* Actually, I've come to talk to the rest of your family, as well as the servants.

LULA. Surely you're not implying that someone in this household kidnapped Edward!

SAM. *(pulling a notepad out of his pocket)* No, I'm not saying that at all. I just need some clues to go on. I'm kind of stuck. Too bad that solving cases isn't like solitaire. *(adding confidentially)* You can cheat at solitaire, you know.

JUNIOR. *(angrily)* Who is this moron? *(to* LULA*)* I thought you said you hired the best in the business!

SAM. *(defensively)* She did, Sonny, and who are you?

JUNIOR. I'm Edward Baum-Schell.

SAM. *(looking at* JANE*)* Well, I guess that fixes that. Case's solved. *(starts to exit)*

JUNIOR. I'm Edward Baum-Schell Jr., you idiot. Edward Baum-Schell Sr. is my father.

SAM. I knew that.

JANE. *(stepping forward)* I'm Mr. Spud's assistant, Miss Reynolds. *(looks at* PHOEBE *and and* LULA*)* Perhaps we could speak to Mr. Baum-Schell in private.

LULA. My stepson and I are very close, Sam. I don't think it's a good idea to split up our family during this very stressful time.

JANE. *(briskly)* It'll only be for a few minutes, Mrs. Baum-Schell. Now if you'll excuse us, we have a case to solve. *(pushes* LULA *towards the door)*

LULA. *(haughtily)* Come, Phoebe. We'll go have some break-fast while we wait.

(LULA *and* PHOEBE *exit.*)

JUNIOR. I think I have you figured out. *(folds his arms)* You're one of those fly-by-night private detectives that's more interested in making a fast buck than solving a case. You feed off of people's misery, don't you, Mr. Spud?

SAM. Oh yeah? And I have you all figured out – Junior. You're one of those university jock types. All brawn and no brains – am I right?

JUNIOR. On the contrary, I am an honours student, Mr. Spud. My father bribed the football coach to put me on the team.

SAM. Oh.

JANE. Both of you, stop this! It's getting us nowhere!

JUNIOR. You're right, Miss Reynolds. Now, detective, did you want to ask me some questions about my father?

SAM. *(sprawling on the couch)* Yeah, for starters, did you know that he was planning to cut you out of his will?

JUNIOR. Where did you hear that? That's a lie! A bald-faced lie! Father would never do that!

JANE. Well, someone thinks he would. We heard it from a reliable source, Mr. Baum- Schell.

JUNIOR. I still don't believe it!

SAM. *(pulling the etch-a-sketch out of his pocket)* It's the truth, Junior. *(turns the knobs a few times and holds it out to* **JUNIOR***)* Do I have to draw you a picture?

JUNIOR. *(shoving* **SAM** *aside)* Get that away from me!

JANE. Do you know of anyone who would kidnap your father, Mr. Baum-Schell?

JUNIOR. My father had lots of enemies – Mr. Alpo, Mr. Kennel Ration, Mr. Kibbles and Bits. They all hated him.

SAM. Where were you on the night of the kidnapping?

JUNIOR. I was out shopping at my favourite health food store. I've been trying to increase my bone mass, and I'd heard that these new calcium supplements might do the trick.

SAM. Yeah, whatever, so can anyone back up your story?

JUNIOR. Well – the lady at the health food store might remember me.

SAM. *(to* **JANE***)* Make a note to check out his alibi. *(to* **JUNIOR***)* Now, can you tell me why you had your father kidnapped?

JUNIOR. I just told you I was at the health food store!

JANE. Sam, what are you doing?

SAM. *(to* **JANE** *in a loud whisper)* I'm using my surprise question technique, kid. It never fails. If the guy's the culprit, he crumbles like a graham wafer.

JANE. And what if he doesn't?

SAM. Then he's a really good liar.

JANE. *(pushing him aside)* You better let me take over. *(to* **JUNIOR***)* Is there anything that's happened in the last few days that strikes you as strange, Mr. Baum-Schell?

JUNIOR. Am I ever glad you asked that question, Miss Reynolds! *(looks nervously at the door)* It's my stepmother. She pretends to be upset about my father's kidnapping, but I don't buy it. She's been after his money from the very beginning. And my sister Phoebe –

SAM. Now there's a hardened criminal if I ever saw one!

JANE. She's a school girl, Sam!

SAM. You don't know how tough schoolgirls can be, Jane. Why, when I was in Grade Seven –

JUNIOR. *(looking at his watch)* Look, if the two of you are done interviewing me, I'd really like to have my breakfast and hit the gymnasium.

SAM. Do you work out on the pommel horse, Mr. Baum-Schell?

JUNIOR. No – the rings. *(flexes his muscles to demonstrate then begins to exit)*

JANE. Do you think you could send in your sister on your way out? We'd like to question her as well.

JUNIOR. Of course. Oh, and Mr. Spud? I'd like you to know that if my father dies as a result of your bungling this case, I will personally thrash you within an inch of your life. Do I make myself clear?

(JUNIOR exits.)

SAM. Well, what do you think, Jane? He looked guiltier than a five year old with his hand in the cookie jar.

JANE. If anything, Sam, we should be having a closer look at Lula.

SAM. Lula? How can you say that? She hired me in the first place!

JANE. Look at this house, Sam. It reeks of money. And that woman wants it all to herself, I just know it. I think we had better watch Lula very carefully from now on.

(Blackout.)

Scene Five

(*Livingroom of the Baum-Schell mansion. Just before midnight.*)

(**PHOEBE, LULA,** *and* **JUNIOR** *are seated on the couch.* **JANE** *is standing at the window.* **MARTHA** *is seated at the desk, reading the ransom note. Beside the desk is a briefcase.* **SAM** *stands near the exit.*)

JANE. Now is everyone clear on the procedure for tonight?

SAM. *(raising his hand uncertainly)* Can you just repeat the part you said after – now listen carefully?

JANE. We don't have time for that, Sam. It's nearly midnight. Now I want you all to vacate this room until I give the signal. I don't want anyone to stumble in here by accident and get shot by the kidnappers.

PHOEBE. Are you sure your plan will work, Miss Reynolds?

JANE. No, Phoebe, but we've got to try something. If we just hand over the money to the kidnappers, they'll kill your father for sure.

SAM. *(wisely)* Dead men tell no tales.

LULA. *(pointing to the briefcase)* Are you sure all the money is there? When I took it from the bank this afternoon, I didn't have time to count it.

JANE. It's all there, Mrs. Baum-Schell. One million dollars.

MARTHA. *(taking off her glasses and setting them on the desk)* The note says that the briefcase should be left on the desk. Shouldn't we move it?

JANE. *(placing the briefcase on the desk)* There. Thank you for reminding me.

JUNIOR. Are you sure we shouldn't call the police? They know how to handle these situations.

SAM. And I don't?

JUNIOR. *(standing up)* You have my point exactly.

(**JANE** *steps in between them.*)

JANE. Mr. Baum-Schell, the time has come for you to retire to your room. And that goes for the rest of you. Turn off the lights upstairs and wait.

(**LULA, PHOEBE, SAM, MARTHA,** *and* **JUNIOR** *get up to leave.*)

JANE. Sam, you stay here, remember!?

SAM. *(shrugging)* Oops.

(**LULA, PHOEBE, MARTHA,** *and* **JUNIOR** *exit.*)

JANE. Now, the ransom note said to turn off all the lights in the room. We'll just hide behind these curtains until they come.

(**JANE** *and* **SAM** *move behind the curtains.* **JANE** *turns off the lights.*)

(*Blackout.*)

SAM. *(after a moment)* I sure wish I had Binky.

JANE. Sam, don't be ridiculous! You're a grown man! Here – hold my hand if it'll make you feel any better.

SAM. Thanks, kid.

JANE. You know, Sam, there's something I've been meaning to tell you. It's something I should have told you a long time ago, but I just didn't have the nerve.

SAM. It's okay, kid. I know already.

JANE. *(surprised)* You do? But how did you ever figure it out?

SAM. Let's just say – a little bird told me.

JANE. He did? When?

SAM. Sssh! I think someone's coming!

(*A figure enters, carrying a flashlight. The flashlight swings around the room and then falls on the briefcase on the desk. The figure crosses the room towards the desk.* **SAM** *grabs the figure's outstretched arm, while* **JANE** *turns on the lights.*)

JANE. Phoebe!

SAM. I told you she was the crook!

PHOEBE. *(struggling to free her wrist from Sam's grasp)* It's not how it looks! I'm not a kidnapper! I'm just a – a kid!

SAM. *(smugly)* Then how do you explain coming in here and trying to grab this suitcase full of money, eh? Need a little extra spending money for the mall perhaps?

PHOEBE. No, I didn't come back for the money – just for my Nancy Drew book. See, it's here on the desk – where I left it this morning. *(to* JANE*)* I always read Nancy Drew before I go to bed. *(shows* SAM *the book)* It's *The Mystery of the Old Clock*! I was going to read it under the covers – with my flashlight!

SAM. A likely story! Wait until I get you down to the station! One hour in the cooler and you'll crack like a walnut!

JANE. *(shaking her head)* Sam, can't you see that she's telling the truth? This girl's no kidnapper. *(to* PHOEBE*)* Take your book and go up to your room, Phoebe. And don't come back in here until I give the signal, okay?

*(***PHOEBE*** nods obediently and exits with her book tucked under her arm.)*

JANE. Now, shall we try again?

*(***JANE*** turns out the lights. She and* ***SAM*** *resume their places behind the curtains.)*

SAM. I still think you're making a mistake. That girl has trouble written all over her.

JANE. Sam, you are a lousy judge of character.

SAM. I like you, don't I?

JANE. You do?

SAM. Sure, kid. I think you're swell. In fact, when this is all over, maybe you and me could go to a movie some night.

JANE. Ssssh! Somebody's coming!

(A figure enters with a flashlight and surveys the room, much like the first time. The figure moves toward the desk. ***SAM*** *leaps out from behind the curtains again.* ***JANE*** *turns on the lights.* ***SAM*** *is holding* ***MARTHA*** *by the arm.)*

JANE. Martha!

SAM. I knew it was you all along!

MARTHA. *(crying out in pain)* Take your hands off me, young man! You're hurting me!

SAM. Sure, I'll take my hands off you – when you tell me where you've stashed your boss!

MARTHA. I have no idea where Mr. Baum-Schell is, you idiot! I just came down here for my glasses. I left them here on the desk. Can't see a blessed thing without them!

SAM. A likely story, you old bat!

JANE. Sam, I think she's telling the truth. *(picks up the glasses and hands them to **MARTHA**)* Here you are, Martha. I'm sorry that Sam roughed you up.

MARTHA. *(putting on her glasses and looking at **SAM** reproachfully)* Whom are you calling an old bat?! I've a good mind to teach you some manners!

SAM. Hey, I'm sorry, all right?

JANE. *(ushering **MARTHA** out of the room)* Now you go back upstairs, Martha and please don't come back in here until I give the signal.

*(**MARTHA** exits.)*

SAM. *(pointing to the curtains)* Shall we?

JANE. I just hope we haven't scared off the real kidnappers with these house lights going off and on like a pinball machine. *(turns out the lights)*

SAM. You're my kind of girl, kid.

JANE. Ssssh! Someone's coming!

SAM. Oh brother!

*(The door opens and a figure enters, carrying a flashlight. The flashlight pans the room and falls on the briefcase on the desk. The figure crosses the room and grabs the briefcase. **SAM** grapples with the figure and **JANE** turns on the lights. The figure is **JUNIOR**. **LULA** is standing at far left, holding a revolver and wearing the trench coat.)*

JANE. Junior!

SAM. I knew it was him! *(excitedly to* JANE*)* Didn't I say it was him?!

JUNIOR. *(struggling)* You better let go of me, Spud! I'm on the boxing team as well as the football team!

SAM. I'm so afraid.

LULA. *(cocking the revolver)* I'd let him go, if you know what's good for you, Sam.

SAM. Lula!

JANE. She's got a gun, Sam. You better do as she says.

> (SAM *releases* JUNIOR. LULA *motions for* SAM *to go stand beside* JANE *at the window.* JUNIOR *picks up the briefcase and backs towards* LULA.*)*

LULA. And neither of you ever suspected little old me? How quaint!

JANE. I did – from the first moment you walked into Sam's office. I thought you were as phoney as that bleached blonde hair of yours.

LULA. *(angrily)* Suppose you tell me what my plan is then?

JANE. Well – I'd say that you had Junior go along with his father the other night when he went out to his men's club. Junior knocked out Edward in the garage and dragged him into the gym. If we checked the equipment room, we'd probably find him in there somewhere.

SAM. *(snapping his fingers)* That's why he was always going to the gym! To check on his father! *(to* JUNIOR*)* He's still alive, isn't he?

JUNIOR. *(insulted)* Of course he is. He's in perfect health.

LULA. But not for long, if you get my drift. *(reaches into the pocket of her coat and pulls out a syringe)* One shot of this and his heart will stop like a – like a –

SAM. *(helpfully)* Like a school bus at a railway crossing?

LULA. Yes, thank you, Sam.

JANE. But won't an autopsy reveal that Edward died from

this drug?

LULA. It's not detectable by normal forensic methods, Miss Reynolds. To the police, it will appear that Eddie died of natural causes – brought on by the stress of the kidnapping.

JANE. But why did you involve us in your scheme?

LULA. Naturally I didn't want the police involved. They would have seen through all of this immediately.

SAM. Oh.

JANE. But why did you kidnap Edward in the first place? Couldn't you just have convinced him to change his will?

JUNIOR. That's where things become complicated. Two weeks ago Dad discovered that I got kicked off the football team. Even Dad's money wasn't enough for the coach to keep me around. Dad was such a great football player in college that he couldn't stand the thought of his son being a failure on the field. He planned to cut me out of the will, so only Phoebe would inherit. Don't you think I have good reason to hate my father, Mr. Spud?

LULA. And Edward found out that I wasn't quite divorced from my first husband. Legally, Edward and I are not really married. I needed to get rid of Edward before he cut ME out of the will.

SAM. So now what?

LULA. Isn't it obvious? The two of you tried to stop the kidnappers from picking up the money. Junior will take you for a little ride, but you won't be coming back.

JANE. But what about Phoebe? And Martha?

JUNIOR. They're both upstairs – waiting for your signal. By the time they decide to come down, you'll be – *(makes a throat cutting gesture)*. After you're gone, we'll phone the police of course – and tell them how you bungled the money exchange and got shot by the kidnappers.

JANE. *(to* JUNIOR*)* So why were you always talking about

calling the police – if you didn't really want to involve them?

JUNIOR. *(pointing to his head)* Reverse psychology. I learned about it in psychology class.

LULA. Good for you. And now – if you'll come this way – slow and easy. We'll go out to the car.

JANE. *(stalling)* But what about Edward's body?

LULA. I'll take care of him – while Junior's taking care of you. The police will find him tomorrow – according to the directions contained in this note from the kidnappers.

(LULA pulls a piece of paper out of her pocket.)

JANE. Before we leave, can I just ask Junior one thing?

JUNIOR. Go ahead – but it won't do you any good.

JANE. When we interviewed you yesterday, you kept trying to cast suspicion on Lula – saying that she didn't seem very upset by her husband's kidnapping. Were you just trying to throw us off?

LULA. *(looking at JUNIOR suspiciously)* Yes, exactly what were you doing, Junior?

JUNIOR. Nothing, Lula. You have to believe me. They're just trying to make you doubt me – so they can stall for more time.

LULA. You wouldn't try to double-cross me, would you Junior? *(raises the revolver and points it at him)*

JUNIOR. Don't shoot, Lula!

(JANE looks out the window.)

JANE. I don't know if either of you are interested in this, but there's a police car pulling up.

LULA. *(scoffing)* As if I'd fall for that old trick!

SAM. *(looks out the window)* Okay, you don't have to believe her, but don't be surprised if the police walk in here any minute. *(to JANE)* How come they're here?

JANE. It's a long story. I'll explain later.

LULA. *(gesturing with the revolver)* Quit stalling. The three of you can precede me out of here.

JUNIOR. But Lula –

LULA. Be quiet, Junior! Walk!

(Inspector **OISEAU** *enters, surprising* **LULA.** *He grabs the gun out of her hand before she can do anything and trains it on* **LULA** *and* **JUNIOR.***)*

OISEAU. Now, what's going on here?

SAM. Nice of you to drop in, Oiseau.

JANE. Your timing is perfect! These two kidnapped Edward Baum-Schell and planned to murder him – and us. He's in the gym equipment room – probably drugged.

SAM. How come you're here?

OISEAU. I had a phone call from my cousin earlier today – saying zat I better come by zee Baum-Schell estate shortly after midnight.

SAM. *(mystified)* Your cousin?

OISEAU. *(gesturing at* **JANE***)* Jane Reynolds – your secretary. She's my cousin. *(pulls a walkie-talkie out of Lula's trench-coat pocket and talks into it)*

SAM. *(to* **JANE***)* You're his cousin?!

JANE. Third cousins actually. Twice removed. I tried to tell you – and you said you already knew!!

*(***OISEAU** *shrugs and begins putting handcuffs on* **LULA** *and* **JUNIOR.** *He makes her take off her coat first and hang it on the coat rack.)*

OISEAU. Looks like you owe me one, Spud.

SAM. Looks like we're EVEN, you mean.

OISEAU. Whatever. I've radioed my partner to go pick up Baum-Schell from zee gym. Do you need any more assistance?

JANE. No, we'll be fine. Thanks, Quincy.

SAM. *(smiling)* Quincy? Your first name is Quincy?

OISEAU. Oui.

*(**MARTHA** *and* **PHOEBE** *enter)*

JANE. Phoebe! We forgot all about you and Martha!

PHOEBE. *(looking around curiously)* I heard Lula and Junior shouting – so I thought I should come downstairs. I went to get Martha first. What's going on here? I am so confused.

MARTHA. *(looking at* LULA *contemptuously)* Is there anything I can get for you, Madame?

LULA. *(sarcastically)* Not at the moment. I'll keep you posted.

(MARTHA *and* PHOEBE *cross to far R.* MARTHA *sits at desk.* PHOEBE *sits on the couch.)*

OISEAU. *(to* PHOEBE*)* This woman is under arrest for kidnapping and attempted murder.

PHOEBE. And Eddie?

OISEAU. I'm afraid zat he is an accomplice, young lady. *(pauses)* And you are?

PHOEBE. *(looking smug)* The heiress to a pretty big estate, I imagine.

(CONSTABLE *and* EDWARD BAUM-SCHELL *enter.)*

PHOEBE. *(leaping to her feet and running to embrace her father)* Daddy!

EDWARD. *(hugging her)* Hello, my angel.

JANE. Mr. Baum-Schell, I presume?

EDWARD. Exactly. And are you the detective who brought about my release?

(PHOEBE *clings to her father possessively)*

SAM. *(stepping forward)* That would be me. My name is Sam Spud, and this woman is Jane Reynolds – my partner.

(JANE *looks surprised.)*

EDWARD. I am deeply in debt to both of you then. If not for you, my faithless wife and son would have done away with me. *(looks at* LULA *and* JUNIOR *in disgust)*

LULA. You want to know why I did it, Edward?

EDWARD. I know why you did it, Lula. You're heartless, manipulative, and greedy.

LULA. You forgot bored. I was bored living here with you! You're boring, Edward!

EDWARD. You think life here is boring? Wait till you see the women's wing of the state penitentiary!

JUNIOR. *(groveling)* I'm really sorry, Dad. Lula made me do it! *(to* **LULA***)* It's all your fault!

EDWARD. Shut up, Junior – before I decide NOT to pay for your defence attorney. *(to* **SAM***)* I hope there is some way that I can repay you, Mr. Spud.

OISEAU. *(ingratiatingly)* I am Inspector Oiseau, Mr. Baum-Schell. If you're up to it, I'd like to take you down to zee station, so zat I can get your statement.

EDWARD. Of course, Inspector. *(looks down at the briefcase)* This is the million dollar ransom?

LULA & JUNIOR. *(disgustedly)* Yes.

EDWARD. *(picking up the briefcase and handing it to* **SAM***)* Will this be enough payment for your services?

SAM. *(coughing in surprise)* Probably.

OISEAU. If I hadn't walked in at zee right moment, these two would have disposed of you, Mr. Baum-Schell as well as Spud and his partner.

EDWARD. And your point is, Inspector?

OISEAU. Well, I –

EDWARD. Has it escaped your notice that someone with these investigative abilities should be working for the police, Inspector? Why isn't this man on the force?

OISEAU. Well, I –

EDWARD. *(to* **SAM***)* The commissioner is a good friend of mine. I'll be speaking to him about this matter to-morrow.

SAM. *(stupified)* Thank you.

OISEAU. *(grumpily)* Let's get down to zee station. It's going to be a long night.

EDWARD. *(bowing)* Good night, Mr. Spud. Miss Reynolds.

SAM. Good night, Mr. Baum-Schell. Good night – Quincy.

(**OISEAU** *gives* **SAM** *a dirty look.* **OISEAU** *and* **CONSTABLE** *exit with* **LULA** *and* **JUNIOR**. **EDWARD**, **MARTHA**, *and* **PHOEBE** *follow.*)

JANE. Did you mean what you said to Mr. Baum-Schell – about me being your partner, Sam?

SAM. Sure, kid.

JANE. But what about getting back on the force?

SAM. *(waving his hand)* I never really liked being a cop. I think I'll stick to being a private eye. From now on the sign on our door will read "Spud and Reynolds –We've Got Eyes for You." What do you think?

JANE. I think you'd better put me in charge of sign painting. And managing our bank account. *(takes briefcase from* **SAM***)* Let's go get a coffee at Danny's Diner and talk about our partnership. *(heads towards the door)*

SAM. *(hesitating)* Hey, when we were behind the curtains – I thought you were trying to say you had a crush on me.

JANE. Sam!

SAM. Do you? *(puts on trenchcoat)*

JANE. Well – you're a hopeless detective – but you're kind of cute.

SAM. *(smiling in satisfaction)* I knew you had a crush on me. *(punches* **JANE** *gently in the jaw)* Here's looking at you, Kid.

(Blackout)

SET

<u>Scene One</u>
Wooden desk
Two chairs
Phone
Coat rack
Window
Door frame

<u>Scene Two</u>
Street lamp

<u>Scene Three</u>
Counter top
cash register
Two stools
One table and 2 chairs
Coat rack
Napkin dispensers
Sugar dispensers
Menus

<u>Scene Four</u>
Desk
chair
Lamp
Coat rack
Window with curtains
Love seat
Phone

<u>Scene Five</u>
Desk
chair
Lamp
briefcase
Coat rack
Curtains
Love seat
Phone

PROPERTIES

Sam Spud
Teddy bear
Magnifying glass
Newspaper
Water pistol
Dart gun
Skipping rope
Etch-a-sketch
Quarter
Mickey Mouse watch
Notepad and pencil
Trenchcoat

Oiseau
Handcuffs (2 pair)

Lula
Lipstick
Compact/mirror
Purse (clutch)
Handkerchief
ring
Gun
Syringe

Phoebe
Nancy Drew book
flashlight

Laverne
watch
police badge
Jane
umbrella
purse

Junior
towel
glasses

Doris
coffee cup
dishtowel
coffee pot
pad of paper/pen
apron

Danny
dish towel
apron
chef's hat

Martha
reading glasses

Superintendent
wrench

COSTUMES

Sam Spud
dark pants
dark shoes
white shirt
black tie (clip on)
detective hat

Jane Reynolds
pumps
blazer
skirt
hat
blouse

Lula Baum-Schell
Scene 1
Black dress
Black pumps
Black hat
Black purse
Mink stole
White gloves
Scene 4
elegant robe and pajamas or
nightgown
Scene 5
Trenchcoat
Hat

Phoebe
White blouse
Paid skirt/jumper
white knee socks
saddle shoes (black and white,
laces)

Junior
Scene 4
sweat pants
running shoes
sweat shirt (wet)
Scene 5
lettered cardigan
black bow tie
white shirt
dark pants
dark shoes

Inspector Oiseau
white shirt
tie
dark pants
suit jacket/blazer
hat
dark shoes

Martha
Scene 4
housecoat
slippers
curlers
Scene 5
white blouse
black skirt
grey wig (or put hair in a bun and
powder)

Superintendent
coveralls

Light Fingers Laverne
gaudy dress and shawl

Edward Baum-Schell
white shirt (looks like he has
been wearing it for several days)
dark pants
dark shoes
tie (worn askew)

Second Story Sid
dark knitted toque
dark turtleneck
dark pants

Benny the Fence
Dark shirt
Bright tie
Suit jacket
light coloured pants
slicked back hair

Police constable
dark pants
white shirt
policeman's cap
dark suit jacket/blazer

OTHER TITLES AVAILABLE FROM BAKER'S PLAYS

KEEPSAKES

Pat Cook

Drama / 4m, 6f / Interior

Ever look at a family portrait and wonder what those people, posed and smiling, are really like? This family portrait shows you the inner workings of the Rogers family – how they deal with everyday things, how they deal with both happy and sad events which effect each and every one of them. These funny, poignant and all-too-human characters go through life the best way they know how.

Austin does his best to keep the house running smoothly, unless he has to take Pawpaw's trunk out of the basement. Mary Jo is outwardly pleased when son Mitchell gets engaged to Tish but explains "They're too young!" Her sister, Brenda, helps out by saying "Not any younger than you were when you got married." Brenda's husband, Dale, has his own advice for young Mitchell – "Marriage consists in large part of just giving up!" And Pawpaw keeps hearing voices and seeing people who aren't there.

The very fabric of the family unit meets its ultimate challenge when Brenda and Dale have to move in with them. Daughter Jan has to put up with a whiney dog, Mitchell and Tish can't seem to find time to talk about their upcoming marriage and everyone is bunking up with everyone else, leaving the men to sleep on the couch – any of this sound familiar? Brought to you by the same author of *Good Help is So Hard to Murder.*

BAKERSPLAYS.COM